PUFFIN BOOKS

Mr Majeika on the Internet

Humphrey Carpenter is the author of the Mr Majeika
stories for children. He was born and educated in
Oxford and worked for the BBC before becoming a
full-time writer in 1975. He has published award-
winning biographies of J. R. R. Tolkien, C. S. Lewis,
W. H. Auden, Benjamin Britten and others, and is the
co-author, with his wife Mari Prichard, of *The Oxford
Companion to Children's Literature*. From 1994 to 1996
he directed the Cheltenham Festival of Literature. He
has written plays for radio and the theatre, including
a dramatization of *Gulliver's Travels* (1995), and for
many years ran a young people's drama group, the
Mushy Pea Theatre Company. He has two daughters.

Humphrey Carpenter

Mr Majeika on the Internet

Illustrated by Frank Rodgers

PUFFIN BOOKS

Published by the Penguin Group
Penguin Books Ltd, 80 Strand, London WC2R 0RL, England
Penguin Putnam Inc., 375 Hudson Street, New York, New York 10014, USA
Penguin Books Australia Ltd, Ringwood, Victoria, Australia
Penguin Books Canada Ltd, 10 Alcorn Avenue, Toronto, Ontario, Canada M4V 3B2
Penguin Books India (P) Ltd, 11 Community Centre, Panchsheel Park, New Delhi – 110 017, India
Penguin Books (NZ) Ltd, Cnr Rosedale and Airborne Roads, Albany, Auckland, New Zealand
Penguin Books (South Africa) (Pty) Ltd, 24 Sturdee Avenue, Rosebank 2196 South Africa

Penguin Books Ltd, Registered Offices: 80 Strand, London WC2R 0RL, England

www.penguin.com

First published 2001

Text copyright © Humphrey Carpenter 2001
Illustrations copyright © Frank Rodgers 2001
All rights reserved
4
The moral right of the author and illustrator has been asserted

Set in 14/22 Palatino

Made and printed in England by Clays Ltd, St Ives plc

British Library Cataloguing in Publication Data
A CIP catalogue record for this book is available from the British Library

ISBN 0–141–31010–3

Contents

1. Hamish Goes Online

"I have some exciting news for you all,"
Mr Potter, the head teacher, told the
whole of St Barty's School at assembly
one Monday morning. "We've been given
a present of computers. There will be one
for each class."

Everyone cheered, even Hamish
Bigmore, the worst-behaved boy in Class
Three. "Hooray for computers!" he
shouted. "They're much better than
boring old books."

Mr Potter went on: "The computers are

a gift from a business just down the road from the school. They're installing new ones, so they've given us their old computers as a present."

Hamish stopped cheering. "We don't want old computers," he grumbled. "We want new ones, like my computer at home. It's a mega-giga-bigger machine than any of you lot have got," he sneered at the rest of Class Three. "I can play computer games, download pop music off the Internet and watch a film all at once," he boasted.

"How silly," said Thomas, and his twin, Pete, said: "What's the point of doing three things at once on a computer, Hamish?" But in truth Thomas and Pete both felt jealous of Hamish's expensive new computer. At home, they had to share an old one with their father and mother, and it couldn't do any of the things that Hamish had talked about.

"We don't have a computer in our house," said Jody. "My mum and dad don't like them."

"How silly can you get?" mocked Hamish as they walked across to Class Three's classroom. "If you don't have a computer, nobody can send you an e-mail. I get e-mails from all over the world," he went on. "All sorts of famous people write to me at my e-mail address."

"Let me guess what your e-mail address is, Hamish," said Pete. "How about *Hamish@stupid.idiot.uk,*" he suggested, dodging out of the way as Hamish tried to kick him.

In the classroom, Mr Majeika was peering at the computer which had been given to Class Three. "I haven't the faintest idea how to work it," he said.

"It's easy-peasy," said Hamish. "So easy that all the other teachers can do it standing on their heads."

"Oh, is that how you do it?" said Mr Majeika, and he flew up in the air and zoomed down so that he landed on his head. Before Mr Majeika became a teacher he had been a wizard, and he still did some rather odd and magical things.

Hamish ignored the upside-down Mr Majeika, and sat down at the computer. He typed on it, clicked the mouse, looked at the screen, and soon got very cross. "This is a useless, rubbishy old machine," he said. "It takes hours and hours to do anything. My computer can zap around the Internet at twice the speed of lightning, but this one is like a creaky old bike with a flat tyre."

"Perhaps, Mr Majeika," said Jody, "you could magic it so that it will work faster?"

Mr Majeika shook his head sadly. "I'm afraid not, Jody," he said. "I don't have any spells that would work on computers. They're far too modern for my magic to have any effect on them."

Just then Mr Potter came into the classroom. "I forgot to mention something else about the new computers," he said. "The school needs to have its own web site, so I'd like everyone to have a go at designing it. We'll put the class's winning entry on the Internet."

"What's a web site?" asked Mr Majeika when Mr Potter had gone. "Is it something to do with spiders?"

"No, Mr Majeika," explained Thomas, laughing. "It's a bit like a book or a magazine, but you read it on the computer screen."

"And what's that net thing Mr Potter was asking about?" said Mr Majeika. "Is it something to do with fishing?"

Jody, Thomas and Pete tried to explain to Mr Majeika about the Internet – how you can send and receive messages from all around the world on it, in just a few seconds. But since wizards can travel round the world by magic, very fast indeed, Mr Majeika wasn't impressed. "I can't see the point of computers," he said.

"Still, if Mr Potter wants everyone to design this web thing for the net thing, we'd better have a go."

After a couple of days, most of Class Three had done designs for the web site, working on the class's computer. Melanie's was the prettiest; it had a picture of fleecy lambs frisking around the school gate, beneath which were the words "Come to St Barty's School, where the teachers are the sweetest in the world." Hamish's was the ugliest; it had a picture of Hamish himself, with the words "This is the STAR PUPIL of St Barty's School, well-known celebrity HAMISH BIGMORE, tanned, handsome, six feet three inches tall."

"You're not six feet three inches tall, Hamish," laughed Thomas. "You wouldn't be as tall as that even if you stood on a chair. And I think your web site is stupid."

"Not as stupid as yours, fatface," said Hamish, sticking out his tongue at Thomas. "It's just a boring old map of the school, with silly drawings of the teachers."

Thomas and Pete had worked together on the map and the drawings. The map was a bit peculiar. "We've made the school toilets look bigger than the classrooms," said Pete. And their drawing of Mr Potter made him look like a mad old tramp.

In the end, it was Jody's web site which Mr Potter decided to put on the Internet. It had a very good drawing of Mr Majeika, with the words "Come to St Barty's School, it's really magical!"

Hamish was very cross not to be the winner. Thomas and Pete found him at

Class Three's computer, writing an e-mail to someone, but he wouldn't let them read it.

The next day, when Class Three arrived in the morning, their computer had vanished, and in its place stood a brand new one, twice as big, with an enormous screen. Hamish Bigmore said he didn't know where it had come from. "But he's

STAR PUPIL
of St Barty's School
Well-known celebrity
HAMISH BIGMORE
Tanned, handsome, six feet three inches tall

got a nasty grin on his face," said Jody, "so, Mr Majeika, I think we should be very careful how we use this strange new computer."

2. The Frog-monster and the Mouse

The new computer sat in a corner of the classroom while Mr Majeika started to teach the next lesson. "This term we're going to begin to learn a little geometry," he said. "Geometry is the shape of things. Triangles, for instance." He drew a triangle on the blackboard. "Can anybody tell me how many sides this triangle has got?"

Jody put up her hand and said, "Three."

Mr Majeika nodded, but everybody

started laughing. On the giant screen of the new computer had appeared the words *"Nonsense! Any idiot knows that a triangle has seventeen sides."*

Mr Majeika frowned. "Hamish Bigmore," he said crossly, "are you up to something?"

Hamish shook his head and said, "It's nothing to do with me, Mr Majeika. I haven't touched the computer, have I?"

Mr Majeika tried to get on with the lesson. "If a triangle has three sides," he asked, "how many sides are there in a square?" He drew a square on the blackboard, and everyone called out, "Four sides". But the computer screen was now saying, *"Don't be so stupid! Any fool knows that a square has one million sides."*

"Let's turn the computer off, Mr Majeika," said Pete, and Mr Majeika agreed. But although Pete turned the computer's main switch to "off", and even pulled out the electrical plug from the wall, the machine refused to switch off. *"Silly fools!"* the words on its screen now said. *"However hard you try, you'll never be able to turn me off."*

"Do a spell over it, Mr Majeika," said Jody. "Surely you can think of *some* magic that's powerful enough to stop it being such a nuisance."

Mr Majeika thought for a moment, then he shut his eyes, waved his hands, and muttered the words of a spell.

Everything went black, and there were flashing lights and very odd noises. Class Three felt as if they were being whirled round and round. Then the noises died down, and it started to get light again.

"Phew! That's a relief," said Mr Majeika. "I really didn't think the spell would work. But look, the computer has vanished."

"Wait a minute, Mr Majeika," said Jody. "We can't see the computer, but where do you think we are?"

"In our classroom as usual," said Thomas. "Look, there are the tables and chairs."

"But there's something funny going on," said Pete. "There's a huge window of glass between us and the rest of the room."

"Yes," said Jody, "and if you turn round, what's behind us?" Thomas and Pete turned.

"The whole wall is glowing!" said Thomas.

"And there are giant words on it," said Pete.

"Yes," said Mr Majeika. "It says, '*Ha! ha! You've really gone and done it now, you silly idiot.*'"

"I'm awfully afraid, Mr Majeika," said
Jody, "that your spell has made things far
worse. Don't you realize where we are?
We're inside the computer – between the
glass and the screen! And I don't know
how we'll ever get out."

Melanie started to cry, the way she
always did when something went wrong
in Class Three, and Thomas shouted:
"Look! There's someone who *isn't* inside
the computer."

Sure enough, Hamish Bigmore was still standing in the classroom, on the other side of the glass. They couldn't hear what he was saying, but he was laughing nastily. As they watched, he sat down at the computer and started to type things on the keyboard.

Suddenly the giant screen behind them changed, and on it they could read the giant words *"Come to St Barty's School, it's really magical!"*

"That's the web site you designed, Jody," said Pete. "Perhaps we could find a way out of the computer by exploring it."

"Yes," said Thomas, "the letter 'a' in 'St Barty's' has turned into a door. Let's all walk through it and see what's on the other side." He opened the 'a', and, rather nervously, they all followed him through it.

Inside, it was very dark, but in the

distance they could see a small glowing doorway.

"Let's try that," said Pete. They began walking towards it when suddenly there was a huge whooshing sound and a giant green monster appeared.

Everyone screamed and tried to run away, but just then some bouncy music started to play, and Class Three found they were being lifted up in the air by an invisible force. They landed on the back of the monster, who zoomed off at high speed, carrying them out of the dark place into a strange country full of tall towers and nasty-looking castles.

"Help!" said Jody. "How will we ever get back to school, Mr Majeika?"

The music changed from the bouncy tune and began to sound more frightening, and the green monster stopped zooming around.

"Hey," said Pete, "I recognize these tunes, don't you, Thomas? They're from a computer game we've got at home."

"Yes," said Thomas, "it's a game called 'Zoggo the Frog-monster'. Of course! We've been riding on Zoggo's back!"

"You mean, we're in a computer game?" said Jody.

"Yes," said Pete, "and I think we've just got to the bit where Zoggo is attacked by something much nastier. Oh no! Here it is coming now!"

A huge grey slimy thing was squelching along towards them.

"It's Slime-o the Giant Sea Slug," said Thomas. "Help!"

"We must get out of this game!" said Jody.

"If we're in the game," said Thomas, "someone must be playing it. Oh yes – look! Guess who!"

They looked through the giant glass
screen behind them. Sure enough, there
was the person who was playing the
computer game and giving them all such
a dangerous time – of course, it was
Hamish Bigmore. He was grinning all
over his face.

"What's that he's got on the table,
under his hand?" asked Mr Majeika.

"That's the mouse," said Jody.

"It doesn't look like a mouse," said Mr

Majeika. "It's grey, but it's made of plastic."

"It's called a mouse," Thomas explained, "because it looks a bit like one. It's part of the computer – the part that makes exciting things happen when you move it about and click it. But it's not a real mouse, Mr Majeika."

"Oh, isn't it?" said Mr Majeika. And he shut his eyes and waved his hands. Through the glass they could hear a scream. The computer mouse had turned into a real mouse. Hamish was yelling, because it was a very big mouse, and it had sunk its teeth into his clothes. Before he could get free, it had somehow dragged him through the glass and into the computer.

"How do you do?" said the mouse to Mr Majeika and Class Three.

3. Gulliver Leads the Way

"Thank you for coming to rescuing us," said Jody to the mouse. "Now can we please all get out of this computer?"

The mouse frowned. "I'm afraid you can't," he said. "Or at least, I don't know how you will manage it. You see, computers are worked from the outside, with a mouse like me. But now I'm inside it, with all of you, I'm powerless to help you escape."

Melanie started to cry again. "Boo-hoo! We're going to be in this horrid computer for ever and ever, and I'll never see my mummy and daddy again." And the truth was, the rest of Class Three felt just as miserable.

"What a lot of stupid idiots you are," said Hamish Bigmore, who was starting to recover from his shock. "I think being in a computer is much more exciting than being in a boring old classroom, and having boring old mums and dads collect you from school at the end of the afternoon, so they can take you back to your boring old homes. This is our big chance! We can surf the Internet. We can visit all sorts of places and people right round the world, thanks to the power of electronics. It's far more exciting than your stupid old magic, Mr Majeika."

Mr Majeika looked at the mouse. "What do you think?" he asked. "Could we really do some travelling on that net thing, and maybe, in time, get to somewhere that has a way out of the computer?"

The mouse nodded. "It's not such a silly idea," he said. "I've seen the Internet, from where I used to sit on the desk in front of the computer, but I've never been on it."

"How do we start?" asked Pete. "Perhaps we should shout out the names of the places we want to visit. Some computers can understand human voices, can't they?"

The mouse nodded. "That might work," he said. "By the way, I never introduced myself properly. My name is Gulliver."

"Gulliver?" said Thomas. "I've heard that name somewhere before."

"It's from a famous book called *Gulliver's Travels*," said Jody, "which is about a man who travels to strange lands and meets peculiar people. I've seen it on television. The first place Gulliver goes to is called Lilliput."

"Lilliput?" said Mr Majeika. "Oh, I went there myself, about three hundred years ago. It's full of tiny people – the littlest people you've ever seen. Perhaps they could help us escape from the computer. Why don't we go there right now? We'll all shout the name and see if the computer can hear us."

"Of course it can," said Hamish Bigmore. "A really super-modern computer like this one has 'Voice Recognition', which means you can tell it things and it understands them."

"Excellent," said Mr Majeika. "Come on, everyone."

And all Class Three shouted, at the top of their voices, "Lilliput!"

For an instant nothing happened, then

all of a sudden they seemed to be sailing very fast in a ship. A moment later, it crashed into some rocks, throwing them on to dry land.

The sun was shining very brightly, and they must have been exhausted after their journey at the speed of lightning, because they all fell asleep. When they woke up, Mr Majeika was nowhere to be seen.

"I expect he's gone for a walk," said Jody. "I think we're on a desert island, so maybe he's gone off to explore it. Let's stay where we are until he comes back."

Gulliver the mouse frowned. "I sense danger," he said. "I think we ought to go and look for your teacher." So they set off.

They didn't have far to look. Behind a clump of trees, they saw Mr Majeika lying on the ground, on his back. "Isn't it nice here, Mr Majeika?" called Jody. But Mr Majeika didn't reply, and when they

reached him, they saw that he was tied up
with tiny threads that were binding him
to the ground. Even his mouth was tied so
that he couldn't speak.

"Who's done this, Mr Majeika?" asked
Thomas. But of course Mr Majeika
couldn't answer.

"Look!" said Jody. She'd spotted that, a
little distance away, some very tiny
people, less than a few centimetres high,
were peering out at them from behind a
rock. "This must be Lilliput," said Jody.
She called out to the little people, "We

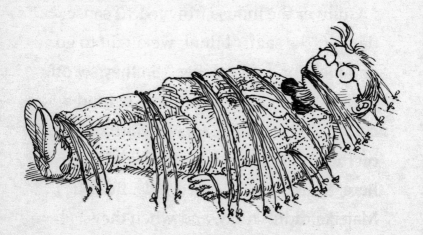

won't harm you, if you'll untie Mr Majeika."

There was a long pause, and then three of the tiny people stepped forward very nervously. "We're sorry to have tied him up," said one of them, "but you see, it's very disturbing having our country invaded by giants like yourselves, who interrupt us at our very important work."

"We're dreadfully busy," said the second tiny person.

"We spend all day at our computers," said the third.

"Oh," said Thomas, "do you have computers too?"

"Of course," said the first Lilliputian. "They're the only thing that makes life worth living. Do you know, computers can send information round the world at three times the speed of light?"

"What sort of information?" asked Pete.

"Oh, all kinds," said the second Lilliputian. "On my computer, for example, I have a list of all the bananas that have ever been grown. I can send it from Lilliput to Honolulu and back again in just over three milliseconds. Isn't that wonderful?"

"Three milliseconds!" mocked the second Lilliputian. "That's ridiculously slow! On my computer, I have a list of all the bricks that have ever been used to build houses. I can send it from Lilliput to Timbuctoo and back again in just over two milliseconds. Isn't that wonderful?"

"Two milliseconds!" mocked the other Lilliputian. "How slow can you get? On my computer, I have a list of all the sneezes that have ever been sneezed. I can send it from Lilliput to the North Pole and back again in less than one millisecond. Isn't that incredible?"

"What a load of rubbish!" laughed Hamish Bigmore. "Who cares how many bananas have ever been grown, or how many bricks have been used to build houses, or how many sneezes have ever been sneezed? You're wasting your time."

"Don't be rude, Hamish," said Jody. "And anyway, what do you use your computer for at home? I've heard you boasting of all the things you've sent to and fro on the Internet, but they don't sound any more sensible to me than what these Lilliput people are doing."

"Please," Pete asked the Lilliputians, "we're trying to get back to St Barty's School. Can you help us?"

The Lilliputians shook their heads. "But we'll untie this giant," they said, pointing at Mr Majeika, "if you'll all go away and leave us alone."

"Of course we will," said Thomas, and

the Lilliputians began the untying. "But
we don't know where to go," said
Thomas. "Who can help us find our way
home?"

"You could go to Brobdingnag, and ask
the people there," answered the first
Lilliputian.

"Brobdingnag?" said Gulliver the
mouse. "All right, we'll try it. Let's all

shout the name, and then the computer will take us there, like it did to Lilliput."

"But wait a moment," said Jody. "I remember that in *Gulliver's Travels*, Brobdingnag is a country full of –"

But it was too late. Everyone else had shouted "Brobdingnag!" and instantly they were whirling through the air.

4. I'm Famous!

"Giants," said Jody, finishing what she'd been saying. "That's what Brobdingnag is full of. We mustn't go there, it might be dangerous."

But they were already there. Behind them, a giant notice board rose into the sky.

"*Welcome to Brobdingnag*," it said, "*the web site where everyone is famous!*"

They picked themselves up, and were starting to look around when they heard giant footsteps. A huge man in an enormous T-shirt and jeans was strolling along. He was followed by another giant, who was holding a camera and taking lots of pictures of him. On the first giant's T-shirt were the words *"I'm famous!"*

When he saw Mr Majeika and Class Three, he waved to them and called out, "Hi there, tiny visitors to Brobdingnag. Pass up your autograph books and I'll sign them for you."

"We don't have any autograph books," said Jody. "We didn't know we were going to meet anyone famous."

"Never mind," said the giant. "Why don't I pick you all up, and then you can be in the photographs with me. When you get back home, you can tell all your friends you've had your picture taken with Famous Fred."

Class Three weren't sure that they

wanted to be picked up, but without
waiting for their answer, Famous Fred
scooped them off the ground into one of
his giant hands. He held them in front of
him, and the photographer took more
pictures.

"What are you famous for?" Thomas
asked Famous Fred.

"It's a bit rude of my brother to ask
that," said Pete, "but you see, we're
strangers to this web site, and we don't
know anybody here yet."

"What am I famous *for*?" echoed
Famous Fred. "What a silly question. I
don't understand it at all."

"Well," said Jody, "take Mr Majeika, for
example. He's famous – at least at St
Barty's School, where we come from – for
doing magic. What have you done that's
made you famous?"

Famous Fred laughed. "Why, I'm

famous for being famous," he said. "What else is there to be famous for?"

"He's the most famous person in Brobdingnag this week," explained the photographer, taking more pictures of Fred. "There are photos of him in all the newspapers and magazines, and he keeps appearing on TV."

"But *why*, you silly idiots?" asked Hamish Bigmore rudely. "Where we come from, you can only get famous by doing something, like being a pop star or a footballer. This is a stupid web site if everyone can become famous for no reason at all!"

"Don't be rude, Hamish," said Mr Majeika.

"And I don't think you're right, Hamish," said Jody. "We've got lots of famous people back home, who seem to be famous just for being famous."

"We're having a party now for all the most famous people in Brobdingnag," said Famous Fred. "I'll take you all along to it. It's at the television studios."

The photographer followed them, still taking pictures, as Fred carried Class Three and Mr Majeika further into the Brobdingnag web site. Other giants passed them by. They wore T-shirts which said things like *"I'm very famous indeed"*, *"I'm even more famous than you"*, and *"I'm the most famous of everyone"*. Each of them was followed by a photographer, taking pictures, and some of them had three or four photographers running after them with their cameras.

Finally they reached a building which said:

BROBDINGNAG TELEVISION STUDIOS – ONLY VERY FAMOUS PEOPLE ARE ALLOWED INSIDE.

Famous Fred walked through the door. "Stop!" shouted a voice. It was a man in a peaked cap. "You can come in, Famous Fred," he said, "but those little people you're holding aren't allowed in. They're not famous."

"Oh," said Fred. "I suppose they aren't. Well, goodbye," he said to Mr Majeika and Class Three, putting them down on the ground. "It was nice meeting you, and I'm sure you're frightfully excited to have met someone as famous as me."

"Wait a minute," said Jody. "I think we

could become famous too. Is there anyone else in Brobdingnag who's as tiny as us?"

Famous Fred thought for a moment. "I'm sure there isn't," he said.

"Then surely we ought to be famous for being the smallest people in the web site," said Jody.

"And Mr Majeika should be famous as the only school teacher who was once a wizard," said Thomas.

"And Hamish Bigmore should be famous for being the nastiest, rudest person in Class Three," said Pete. Hamish stuck out his tongue at Pete, but really he was pleased at being called famous.

"And Gulliver should be famous for being the only computer mouse that can talk," said Jody.

"I was listening to that," said another giant, who had come up behind Famous Fred. "How do you do? My name is

Celebrity Charles, and I run this TV station. You're absolutely right, you should all be famous, and I'm going to make you famous by giving you your own TV show. Let's call it *The Famous Tiny People.*"

"What a good idea," said Famous Fred. "And I can be the presenter."

"No you can't, Fred," said Celebrity Charles. "I'm bored with having you and your stupid friends on my programmes.

These tiny people are right – none of you has done anything to be famous. You're just famous for being famous, and that's stupid."

Famous Fred started to look angry. "You can't keep me off TV," he said. "And you can't keep my friends off it either. Look, here they all come now, and they'll bash your TV station to bits if you don't let all of us on your programmes."

"Couldn't you take a rest from being famous for a bit?" Jody asked Famous Fred.

He shook his head. "Being famous is the only thing that makes life worthwhile," he said.

Celebrity Charles and Famous Fred continued to argue, and it looked as if things could get quite nasty. But at that moment, Mr Majeika called out, "Look! There's a flying saucer!"

5. Party Time

Sure enough, a flying saucer was floating past. Class Three waved and shouted at it, and it landed just outside the Brobdingnag Television Studios. A door opened in the side of it, and two smiling women in air hostess's uniform came out.

"Welcome to the flying land of Laputa," said one of them.

"Laputa!" said Jody. "That's another place in *Gulliver's Travels*, but I can't remember what it's like."

"Let's find out," said Gulliver the mouse.

"We're now boarding for this afternoon's flight," called the second hostess. "Step on board Laputa for the most exciting experience you've ever had."

"Can you take us back to St Barty's School?" asked Thomas.

"We can take you to the land of your dreams," said the first hostess. "This is the last call for boarding, and thank you for choosing to fly Laputa."

Mr Majeika was doubtful, but Hamish Bigmore was already rushing on board, and the others had started to follow him. "Come along, Mr Majeika," said Pete. "It'll take us away from these stupid people who just want to be famous."

As soon as they got on board, the flying island took off again. It seemed to be a hundred times bigger inside than outside. Class Three had expected to see rows of seats, as in a plane, but instead it was a giant shopping centre. Lots of people were walking about, going in and out of the shops. Unlike the tiny Lilliputians and the giants of Brobdingnag, the Laputans were the same size as Class Three, but there was one peculiar thing about them.

Round their necks, each of them wore a chain from which was hanging a large piece of plastic, the size of a notice board. These plastic boards weren't all the same. Some had stripes across them, others had pictures, but all of them had the word CREDIT in big letters.

Jody led the way into one of the shops. It didn't seem to be selling anything that you would really want to buy – just expensive bits and pieces. But the

Laputans were queuing up in dozens to spend their money.

Or rather, they weren't handing over actual money. When they got to the head of the queue, they gave the thing they wanted to buy to the shop assistant, who took hold of the CREDIT notice round the person's neck, and cut a bit off it with a large pair of scissors.

"Excuse me," said Jody to one of the shoppers, "can you tell me about these CREDIT things you all wear?"

The shopper, who was a plump middle-aged woman, looked at Jody in surprise. Jody repeated her question, but the woman shook her head, and pointed to the mobile phone she was holding in one hand.

"I think she means you've got to phone her if you want to talk to her," said Thomas. "Actually, I've noticed that none of the Laputans speak directly to each other. They only talk on the phone."

Jody looked around, and it was true. There were lots of chattering people among the crowd of shoppers, but they were all talking into mobile phones, even if the person they were speaking to was only a tiny distance away.

"I haven't got a mobile phone," said

Jody to the woman, who looked very shocked at this. "Anyway, it's stupid to phone people when they're standing right by you."

"No it's not," said Hamish Bigmore, who had been watching. "Just because you haven't got one, silly old Jody, it doesn't mean that I haven't. It was a present from my parents last birthday." He took his mobile out of his pocket, and handed it to Jody.

The woman showed Jody which number to ring, and soon they were talking to each other on the mobiles.

"I'm sorry not to have answered, dear, when you first spoke to me," said the woman, "but, you see, we Laputans have all had mobile phones for about two hundred years – we're far ahead of the rest of the world in scientific inventions. And since we've been using mobiles for

so long, we've forgotten how to talk to
each other without them."

"That's a pity," said Jody. "Please, could
you tell me about those plastic notices
round your necks?"

"Notices? Those aren't notices," said the
woman. "Those are our credit cards.
Don't you have credit cards where you
come from?"

"Oh yes," said Jody, "but they're not as

big as yours, and children don't have them, only grown ups."

"I've got one!" boasted Hamish Bigmore. "It was a present from my parents last Christmas."

"In Laputa," said the woman, "every baby gets a credit card the moment they're born. And they keep them for the rest of their lives."

"And why do the shop-people cut bits off them when you buy things?" Jody asked.

"Because we're using up bits of our credit."

"You mean, like spending your money?" said Jody, and the woman nodded, though she said, "We haven't had actual money, coins and banknotes, for hundreds of years. We just use the credit cards."

"So what happens," went on Jody,

"when the credit is all used up, and there's no more plastic to cut off the cards?"

"Oh, that never happens," said the woman hastily, and changed the subject. "Are you coming to the party tonight?"

"Is there a party?" said Jody. "We haven't been invited."

"There's a party every night, and all night long, in Laputa," said the woman. "Anyone can go to it, providing they have a credit card to pay for it – and of course we all *do* have credit cards, so we can party all night long."

"Do you often go to the party?" Jody asked.

"Every night," said the woman, yawning. "That's why I'm so tired. I never get any sleep."

"Don't you have a job to do in the daytime?"

The woman laughed. "My job is shopping. It's what everyone's job is in Laputa. We shop till we drop. Shop, shop, shop."

"But what about the people who work in the shops?" asked Jody. "Surely they're doing jobs?"

"Yes," said the woman, "but in their spare time they shop, shop, shop as well."

"So you don't do anything else in Laputa except shop and go to parties?"

"No," said the woman. "Why should we?"

"Doesn't it get very boring after a time?" asked Jody.

Before the woman could answer, a man came up with a big pair of scissors, and snipped a piece of plastic off the woman's credit card. "Why did he do that?" asked Jody. "You weren't buying anything."

"No, but I have to pay for using my

mobile phone," the woman explained. "It's very expensive. If I talked on it all day, I'd soon have no credit left at all. Now I must go and do some more shopping. Goodbye, see you at the party, I hope." And she rushed off, into another shop.

Jody gave Hamish back his mobile. "I don't think I like Laputa," she said. "Just shopping and going to parties – it sounds very boring to me."

"Don't be stupid," said Hamish, "it's the best thing in the world. I'd like to live here for the rest of my life."

Mr Majeika, who had been wandering round, looking at the shops, came over to join them. "I'm rather worried," he said. "Gulliver the mouse has discovered that behind the shops there's something rather horrid going on. Come and see."

They went down a narrow passage, and

at the end of it they suddenly found themselves at the very edge of the flying island. "Look!" said Mr Majeika.

Some policemen were herding a group of men and women into a queue. The people all looked very unhappy. "What's going on?" Thomas asked one of the police.

"Can't you see?" he replied. "Look at their necks." Sure enough, the people in the queue all had round their necks the chain that should hold the credit card. But none of them had a card. "They've all used up their credit," said the policeman. "The last little bits of their cards have been snipped away in the shops. And you're not allowed to live in Laputa without a credit card. So now we're saying goodbye to them." And at that moment, to their horror, Class Three saw that the people at the front of the queue

were being pushed off the edge of Laputa, so that they fell down and disappeared from view.

"You can't do that!" shouted Jody angrily.

"Oh, can't we?" said the policeman. "And where are *your* credit cards?" Of course, neither Mr Majeika nor any of Class Three had giant Laputan credit cards hanging round their necks, and in a moment they too had been herded by the police to the edge of the island. They were given a shove, and found themselves falling down through the sky.

6. Work, Work, Work

The fall did not last for very long, and nobody was hurt, because they landed quite softly in a haystack. When they had climbed off it, and brushed the bits of hay from their clothes, Class Three and Mr Majeika saw that they were in the middle of some peaceful-looking countryside. A group of horses was standing not far off, watching them.

"This looks quite like England," said Thomas. "Surely we can find our way back to St Barty's now, Mr Majeika?"

"I hope so," said Mr Majeika. "But somehow I feel that we're still inside the computer, and that our strange journey hasn't yet come to an end."

They walked across the field towards the horses. "Look, there's a notice," said Pete. It was on a large board at the edge of the field, and it said, "Quiet – exams in progress". When they got closer to the horses, they could see that most of them were very young. They were writing on large sheets of cardboard, spread on the ground in front of them, using specially designed pens that were strapped to their hooves. In charge of them was an older horse, who was walking up and down, making sure they didn't cheat.

"I've never seen horses that could write," said Pete.

"Wait a moment," said Jody. "I've just remembered that in *Gulliver's Travels* there are some very clever horses called Houyhnhmns, who can read and write and talk."

"Hello, there!" Gulliver the mouse called to the group of horses. "My friend here wants to know, are you Houyhnhmns?"

The horses all stopped writing, and the older one said, "Of course we are, but

can't you read the notice? We're doing a very important exam, and you really mustn't disturb us."

"I didn't think horses did exams," said Pete. "I thought it was just humans like us."

"How many exams do *you* have to do?" asked the older Houyhnhmn.

"We don't start doing them properly till we're in our teens," said Thomas. "But when we've begun, we have to do them about once a year."

"Once a year?" said the Houyhnhmn. "Why, that's nothing. Young Houyhnhmns of school age, like these ones, have to do exams every day, from the age of five."

"That sounds dreadful," said Mr Majeika. "When I was a wizard, I only had to do an exam once every hundred years. And when do your young

Houyhnhmns stop having to write exams?"

"When they get jobs," explained the senior Houyhnhmn. "But there aren't enough jobs for everyone, so some Houyhnhmns never stop taking exams. They just go on and on in hopes that one day it may get them a job."

"That sounds dreadful," said Jody. "But I'm sorry – we're interrupting you. We'll go away and leave your pupils to finish the exam."

"It's all right," said the Houyhnhmn. "Time's up," he called to the younger horses. "Stop writing. And for the rest of this afternoon, we'll go into Houyhnhmn City and find out more about the sort of jobs you can apply for when you're older."

"Can we come too?" asked Mr Majeika.

"I don't see why not," said the

Houyhnhmn teacher. "Jump on our
backs, and we'll take you there." So Mr
Majeika, Class Three and Gulliver the
mouse all climbed on to the horses, and
off they went.

It was only a short ride into the city, and
when they got there, it looked just like an
ordinary town, except that all the people

were horses. The Houyhnhmns who were carrying them stopped outside a big office block, with a notice on it saying THE BUSY-BUSY CORPORATION, and Class Three, Mr Majeika and Gulliver the mouse climbed off their backs and followed them inside.

They found themselves in a big room, full of horses sitting at computer screens. "The Busy-Busy Corporation is owned by my brother," whispered the Houyhnhmn teacher, "and he doesn't mind me bringing people in to see it. But you must be very quiet, because everyone is working very hard."

The horses working for the Busy-Busy Corporation were all tapping away at their computers, or talking on the telephone, and most of them looked very tired – they kept trying not to yawn.

In one corner of the room, a meeting

was in progress. One of the horses was reading something aloud, and the ones who were listening to him seemed to be finding it hard to keep awake. "Why are they all so tired?" asked Jody.

"Because they work all day," explained the Houyhnhmn teacher, "and then they have to take work home with them at night, because otherwise there wouldn't be time to finish it. They're all completely exhausted."

Just then, one of the horses in the meeting fell sound asleep, and started snoring. Immediately, two other horses, wearing peaked caps and a sort of stripy uniform, rushed into the room and dragged him out with them, almost before he had woken up.

"Why did they do that?" asked Mr Majeika. "Is it a crime to fall asleep in your country?"

"No," answered the Houyhnhmn teacher, "but there are so many people trying to get jobs that if anyone shuts his eyes for a moment, or shows the slightest sign of not loving every minute of the job, then he or she is thrown out, and someone else gets the job. Look, here comes the replacement for the chap who fell asleep." A young, smart-looking horse was already hurrying into the room. He

joined the meeting with a very eager look on his face.

Jody was frowning. "The Houyhnhmns in *Gulliver's Travels* weren't like this," she said. "They were very sensible – more sensible than the human beings that Gulliver met on his journey. But since those days," she said to the Houyhnhmn teacher, "you've all become such hard workers."

"So has everyone, at home as well as here," said Thomas. "Our dad and mum spend all their time working, and they bring work home at night, just like these horses. And it seems so silly, because there are lots of people who don't have jobs at all. You'd think the work could be divided up equally between everyone, and then there'd be no one without a job, and people wouldn't have to work so hard."

"Hush!" said the Houyhnhmn teacher.

"You mustn't say these things. Working all day and all night is the most important thing in the world to a Houyhnhmn."

"You're stupid," said Hamish Bigmore. "Exams are stupid. Getting jobs is stupid. Working hard is stupid."

The Houyhnhmn looked closely at Hamish. "Oh dear," it said, "why didn't I see that before? This person is clearly a Yahoo."

"There were creatures called Yahoos in *Gulliver's Travels*," said Jody, "but I can't remember what they looked like."

"Yahoos look like human beings," answered the Houyhnhmn. "But they don't want to do exams, or get jobs, or work hard. So we keep them in cages, and use them to pull carts and heavy jobs like that. I'll fetch the security police and get this one taken away right now, and put in a cage."

Before they could stop him, the
Houyhnhmn teacher had pressed an
alarm button, and the two security horses
rushed in and grabbed Hamish Bigmore.
"Oh dear," said Mr Majeika, "I really
don't think that even Hamish deserves to
be shut in a cage." He turned to Gulliver
the mouse. "Can't you do something to
stop this?" he asked.

"The only thing to do in a computer
emergency," said Gulliver, "is to call on

the Webmistress. She's the person who controls the Internet. Come on, everyone, let's shout her name."

And before the two horses could drag Hamish out of the office, the whole of Class Three, Mr Majeika and Gulliver called out, "Webmistress!"

Suddenly everything went dark.

7. W.W.W.

When it started to get light again, they
found they were standing in a long
gloomy passage. It stretched ahead of
them into the darkness, and in the
distance there was a faint glow. There was
no sound to be heard, except a quiet
rustling, like something blowing in the
wind.

"Where are we, Mr Majeika?" asked
Thomas.

"I haven't the faintest idea," said Mr
Majeika, "but I have a feeling that the

Webmistress, whoever she may be, isn't very far away – somewhere round that bend in the passage, I'd guess."

"I'm frightened!" said Melanie, and she started to cry.

"We're all frightened, Melanie," said Jody, "but we can't just go on standing here. We've got to find our way out of this peculiar computer-land, where Mr Majeika's magic doesn't work, and get back home. Come on!"

Jody led the way, followed by Gulliver the mouse, Mr Majeika and the rest of Class Three. After a while, Jody stopped, and looked carefully at the wall of the passage. "What do you think it's made of, Mr Majeika?" she asked. "It looks solid, but I think it's some sort of material, a bit like black velvet. And that's where the rustling noise is coming from – it's blowing about in a breeze."

Mr Majeika put his hand out to touch the wall, but then he suddenly pulled it away again, very fast. "Be very careful, everyone," he said. "I myself may not be able to do magic here, but somebody else is weaving spells. Whatever this wall is made of, it's been created magically. So take care, and don't touch it, whatever you do. And be very quiet."

They tiptoed onwards down the passage, with the wall still rustling alongside them. Suddenly Pete stopped and whispered, "Look!" Hanging on the soft black wall was a large bar of chocolate.

"Yummy," said Hamish Bigmore, stretching out his hand to take it.

"No, Hamish," hissed Mr Majeika. "Whatever you do, don't touch it. I'm sure it's been put there to trap us."

"Rotten old spoil-sport," grumbled Hamish. "How do you know?"

"Weren't you listening to what Mr Majeika said?" asked Jody. "There's some kind of nasty magic going on, and we mustn't touch anything."

Hamish went on grumbling, but a little further down the passage he gave a yelp of delight. "Look," he said, "it's my favourite chewing gum!"

Sure enough, hanging on the wall of the passage was a packet of gum. Once again, Hamish stretched out his hand, and once again Mr Majeika snapped: "No, Hamish! Stand back! Don't you understand? Someone is trying to catch us. If anyone touches anything on the walls, they may not be able to let go of it."

It was then that they heard a groaning noise. A little further down the passage, something much larger than the chocolate or the chewing gum was stuck to the passage wall. It was a person, a gloomy-looking man in a black knitted hat. He was groaning to himself as if he had a bad tummy ache, "Oh, dear, oh dear, oh dear, why was I ever so silly as to be rude to her? Why couldn't I just get on with my job and leave the old so-and-so alone? Why did I have to sing her that silly rhyme?"

"Good gracious," said Mr Majeika, as they came up to the man. "Who on earth are you?"

"I'm not on earth," said the gloomy man. "I'm stuck up on this wall. As to who I am, I spend my life underground, down here in the darkness, and my job is to make tunnels. My name is Mungo the Modem. Do you know what a modem is?"

Mr Majeika shook his head, but Gulliver the mouse said, "Of course I do. It's the part of a computer that connects to the Internet."

"That's what I used to be," said Mungo,
"just an electronic gadget. But then *she*
made me into a person, here in computer-
land, so that I could help her to become
the Webmistress. And now I'm stuck here,
on this horrid sticky wall, for ever and
ever and ever, all because I was rude to
her."

"Can't you get down?" asked Jody.
"We'll help you – give me your hand."

"No," said Mungo the Modem. "Don't touch me, and don't touch the wall, whatever you do. Can't you guess what it's made of?"

"I've no idea," said Mr Majeika, "but it's certainly magic."

"No it isn't," said Mungo. "It's something very ordinary, but there's an awful lot of it. Can't you guess?"

"Give us a clue," said Thomas.

"It was put here by *her*, the Webmistress," said Mungo. "So doesn't that give you a hint?"

"Webmistress," said Jody to herself. "Of course – it's a spider's web!"

"That's right," said Mungo the Modem. "It's a specially strong type of web that grips you horribly tight. Even if you touch me and not the web itself, it'll get hold of you. And she's caught me in it."

"Why?" asked Pete. "Did you annoy her?"

"I'll say I did," answered Mungo. "She had me working day and night for her, connecting her to all sorts of bits of the Internet where no one had ever been before, and she never even said thank you. So finally the day came when I wouldn't do anything else for her, and I was very, very rude to her."

"What did you call her?" asked Jody.

"I said she was a stupid old spider with a face like a bag of rubbish that's been left out in a thunderstorm. It wasn't a very clever thing to say, but she got very cross. So then I was even ruder. I made up a rhyme, and chanted it at her."

"How did it go?" asked Thomas.

"*Incy wincy spider*," chanted Mungo the Modem,

You horrid old bug,
You nasty broomstick-rider,
I hate your ugly mug!
I'll squash your spider's web flat,
And throw it in the ditch,
And smash your ugly black hat,
You stupid old witch."
"I bet she didn't like that," said Pete.
"Of course she didn't," said Mungo.

"She picked me up and threw me at this wall of spider's web, and here I am, stuck for ever and ever. I'm hungry and thirsty but, however hard I struggle, I just can't get free."

"We'll help you," said Thomas.

"No, don't touch me," said Mungo, "or you'll get stuck too. That's how this web works – there must be some kind of magic in it."

"D-d-d-did you say 'spider'?" asked Hamish Bigmore, his teeth chattering nervously. "This W-w-w-webmistress, she's not a spider, is she?"

"Of course she is," said Mungo. "What else would you expect to be at the centre of a world wide web? Because that's what it is, this web – it stretches right round the world, under the ground, and her plan is to catch all her enemies in it."

Mr Majeika was thinking hard. "Does

she have another name, this Webmistress?" he asked Mungo.

"Well," said Mungo, "she wears a big black coat, and on it are the initials 'W.W.'"

"W.W.," repeated Thomas thoughtfully. "Who does that make you think of?"

Suddenly there was a whooshing noise and they all screamed. Around the bend in the passage had leaped a giant black spider. "Yes, my dearies," it hissed, "you're getting very warm – you've almost guessed the right answer. You know that when you use the Internet, you always begin with three initials, W.W.W. Well, what do you think they stand for?"

"World Wide Web, you ugly old spider," said Hamish Bigmore, who seemed to have got some of his nerve back.

"No!" shrieked the spider. "You silly little Hamish, you've got it all wrong. 'W.W.W.' stands for the Web of Wilhelmina Worlock! Tee-hee, my dearies, it's me! Wilhelmina is back again!"

8. The End of the Web

"I might have guessed that it was you behind all this computer nonsense, Wilhelmina," said Mr Majeika. Wilhelmina Worlock was a wicked old witch who was always making a nuisance of herself to Class Three. Her only friend at St Barty's was Hamish Bigmore.

"Nonsense?" cackled Wilhelmina. "Computers aren't nonsense, you silly weasly wizard. If you want to keep up with the real magic these days, Majeika, you've got to get online, and zap about on the Internet. You're a silly old fool not to keep up with the times."

"My magic doesn't work inside a computer," said Mr Majeika glumly. "Does yours, Wilhelmina?"

"You bet it does!" cackled Miss Worlock. "I'll show you all – tee-hee! I'll turn Hamish Bigmore, my star pupil, into a spider just like me."

"No you won't!" screamed Hamish, and he began to run off down the passage. Wilhelmina waved her arms and muttered a spell, and Hamish turned not into a spider, but into a mouse like Gulliver. He ran up and down, squeaking angrily.

"Just as I guessed, Wilhelmina," said Mr Majeika. "Your magic may work inside the computer, but not properly. I bet you that all your spells go wrong."

"Nonsense," shrieked Wilhelmina

Worlock. "And just to prove it, I'll turn you, Majeika, into a fly, and catch you in my spider's web, and eat you up." She waved her arms and muttered another spell. Mr Majeika did indeed turn into a large flying creature, but he wasn't black like a fly, but covered with yellow stripes.

"A wasp!" cried Jody. "That's right, Mr Majeika, you attack her with your sting."

The spider and the wasp began to do battle. Mr Majeika kept diving at Wilhelmina, and threatening her with his sharp sting. But she kept jumping out of the way, and climbing up the walls of the passage with her spider legs. Then she began to tear down the walls themselves – huge, sticky spider webs, which she started to throw over Mr Majeika. Sure enough, he was soon trapped. The harder he struggled, the more he became caught

up in the webs, which started to tighten
around him like ropes.

"Let's chant Mungo the Modem's
rhyme at her," said Pete. He and the
others began to shout,

"Incy wincy spider,
You horrid old bug,
You nasty broomstick-rider,
I hate your ugly mug!

I'll squash your spider's web flat,
And throw it in the ditch,
And smash your ugly black hat,
You stupid old witch."

Miss Worlock became very angry at the rhyme, but she still went on tying up Mr Majeika with her webs.

"We'll save you, Mr Majeika," shouted Thomas and Pete, but they couldn't think what to do. Then they saw that, where the webs had been pulled down off the walls, there was a glowing light, and in a space behind the walls was a giant computer keyboard.

"Gulliver," called Jody to the mouse, who was trying to bite Miss Worlock's legs, "you know all about computers. Isn't there something we can do to escape?"

But it was Mungo who answered. "There's the 'Escape' button. If you press that, you can usually get out of a difficult situation on a computer."

"Quick then," said Jody, "someone please find it and press it." Gulliver ran over to the computer keyboard, and jumped across it to the top left-hand corner, where there was indeed a key marked "ESC".

"Hold on tight, everyone!" he called, and then he jumped on to the button.

Everything suddenly started to spin

round and round. Wilhelmina Worlock's spider-clothes came off and she was just her usual ugly self. Mr Majeika stopped being a wasp and turned into several other creatures – including a tortoise, a small elephant and a polar bear – before becoming himself again. Hamish Bigmore turned back into his usual shape. The spider's-web walls of the passage all collapsed, and Mungo the Modem was free at last – he ran off as fast as his legs could carry him. Wisps of the spider's web were blowing around in the air, and Class Three were frightened that they'd get caught in them. But then they found themselves being tossed up in the air, and when they came down to the ground again they were back at St Barty's School, in their own classroom.

"Well, that was certainly an adventure," said Mr Majeika. "And, thank goodness,

we seem to have left Wilhelmina Worlock
behind in computer-land. I can see now,
Hamish Bigmore, that the whole thing
was some trick that you dreamed up – I
bet it was you who arranged for that huge
computer to take over our classroom, and
I'm sure it was Wilhelmina who sent it."

Hamish said nothing, but his guilty
look showed everyone that Mr Majeika
was right.

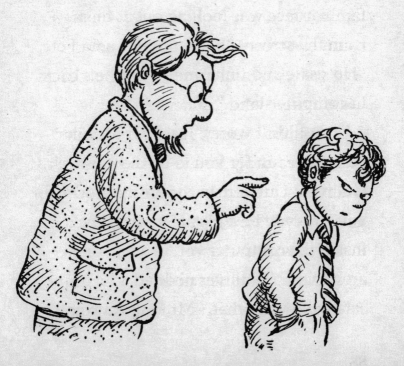

"Where's Gulliver?" said Jody. They looked around, but there was no sign of the mouse. Then they realized that the big new computer had vanished from the classroom, and the old one was back again, with its own mouse attached to it.

"Who wants that stupid old machine?" grumbled Hamish.

Mr Majeika switched it on, and when it had warmed up, to everyone's delight, a familiar face was looking out at them from the screen. "It's Gulliver!" said Pete. "He's safe and unharmed – but he's back in computer-land."

"I shouldn't worry," said Mr Majeika. "It's more fun for you to be there, isn't it, Gulliver? Out here in the ordinary world, you can only be a plastic mouse, but inside the computer you're a real one, aren't you?" Gulliver nodded.

"I'll tell you what," Mr Majeika went

on, "if Hamish doesn't like being back at
school, I'm sure I can magic him inside
the computer again, and then Gulliver
can take him back to the land of the
Houyhnhmns, so he can spend all his
time doing exams." Hamish glared at Mr
Majeika, but he said nothing.

"I've had an idea, Mr Majeika," said
Thomas. "One of the things you can do on

a computer is to minimise things, make them very small, and tuck them away in the corner of the screen while you're doing something else. Why don't you minimise Hamish for the rest of today? That should stop him being a nuisance."

"What a good idea, Thomas," said Mr Majeika. "Hamish, if I hear one more grumble out of you this afternoon, I shall minimise you so that you're very, very tiny. You see, I'm not too old-fashioned to learn from computers after all."